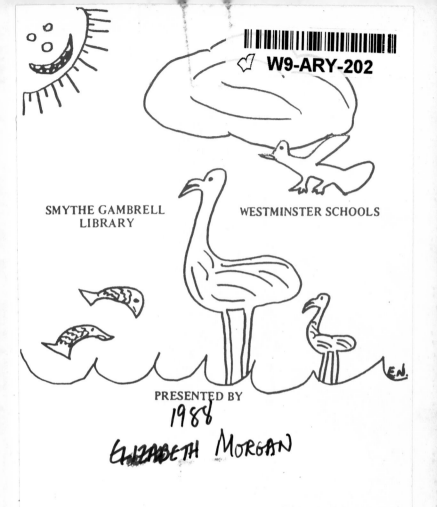

# PET
## D · A · Y

## BY HARRIET ZIEFERT
ILLUSTRATED BY
## RICHARD BROWN

MR ROSE

LITTLE, BROWN AND COMPANY   BOSTON   TORONTO

Sally

# Mr. Rose's Class

Jennifer

Richard

Adam

Emily

Mr. Rose

Matt

Jamie

Kelly

Justin

Sarah

First Edition

Library of Congress Cataloging-in-Publication Data

Ziefert, Harriet.
  Pet Day.

  (Mr. Rose's class)
  Summary: Mr. Rose brings a variety of creatures to his rambunctious
science class on Pet Day and teaches how to handle the little animals.
  [1. Schools—Fiction. 2. Animals—Fiction] I. Brown, Richard Eric,
1946-     ill. II. Title. III. Series: Ziefert, Harriet. Mr. Rose's class.
PZ7.Z487Pe   1987   [Fic]   86-27421
ISBN 0-316-98766-2

Published simultaneously in Canada
by Little, Brown & Company (Canada) Limited

Printed in Singapore for Harriet Ziefert, Inc.

For four teachers of significance—
Stanley Elkins, Janice Gorn,
Morris Meister, Anna Burton

# CHAPTER ONE
# SURPRISE! SURPRISE!

"Good morning, class! It's Monday,"
   Mr. Rose said.
"Good morning, Mr. Rose."
"I know this is Pet Day," said Mr. Rose.
   "Jennifer and Matt have pet stories
      to tell, but first I have an announcement."
"Is it short?" Justin asked.
"Pretty short," Mr. Rose answered.

"Last night, after we left school, one
of the gerbils had babies."

"Ooh, where are they? Can I see?"
Justin asked.

"I wish they'd been born when we were here,"
Kelly said.

"It would have been nice," said Mr. Rose.
"But births don't always happen
when you want them to."

Jamie knew what Mr. Rose was talking about.
She said, "My mother wanted me to be born
in the morning, but I was born in the
middle of the night."

"Me, too," added Kelly.

"I don't know what time I was born," said Sarah.

"You all could ask your parents what time
of day you were born," suggested Mr. Rose.
"Then we could make a graph."

Everyone liked Mr. Rose's idea.

The class would find out whether more children
were born during the day or the night.

"Now can we see the baby gerbils?" Justin asked.

"Yeah," said Richard. "What do they look like?"

"Do they have hair?" someone asked.

"How big are they?"

"Are they pink?"

"Can the babies open their eyes?"

"Can they stand?"

"Do they come from an egg?"

"Wait a minute!" said Mr. Rose. "Too many questions! I'll answer the one about where gerbils come from. When you see the babies, you'll be able to answer the rest."

"But the gerbils are hiding. How can we see them?" Sarah asked.

Mr. Rose promised, "Don't worry, you will. But first, let's talk about eggs and babies."

Jamie, who sometimes liked to show off,
interrupted Mr. Rose.
She announced, "Gerbil babies come from inside
their mothers—like people."
"Right," Mr. Rose said. "All mammals give birth
to live young."
"You mean gerbils are mammals like we are?"
Kelly asked.
"Really?"
"Really," Mr. Rose answered.
"So they don't lay eggs like birds," Kelly said.
Jennifer was confused. "But I read in a book
that a human baby comes from an egg."
"You're right," Mr. Rose said. "But mammals'
eggs are not the same as birds' eggs."

"What do you mean?"

"Birds lay eggs that are hatched outside
the mother's body. Mammals' eggs
grow *inside* the mother's body,"
Mr. Rose explained.

"How long does the egg stay inside the mother?"
Emily asked.

"It's different for each kind of animal.
A gerbil egg grows fast. It only takes
three weeks from the time it is fertilized
by the male until the time of birth."

"Wow! Only three weeks!" Richard exclaimed.

"A human baby takes a long time—nine months,"
Jamie added.

"And an elephant takes even longer!" said
Jennifer, who had just been to the library.

"I want to see the babies," Justin reminded
    Mr. Rose.

"Okay," answered Mr. Rose. "But here are
    the rules."

  Mr. Rose found some chalk and went
    to the board.

"These rules are very important. If they
    aren't followed for at least a week,
    the mother gerbil might become frightened
    and eat her babies."

"That's gross!" said Matt.

"I think it's sad," said Sally.

  Mr. Rose wrote:

*No more than two people at the cage*

*No talking or whispering near the cage*

*No touching any of the gerbils*

*HANDS OFF THE GERBILS*

  *FOR SEVEN DAYS!*

"Remember," Mr. Rose said when he finished
    writing, "a mother gerbil who feels calm
    and safe won't eat her babies."

"Can Emily and I have the first look?"
    asked Jamie.
"That's not fair!" said Justin. "I asked first."
"Well, what's fair?" asked Mr. Rose.
"Alphabetical order," suggested Sarah.
"Okay," said Mr. Rose. "Alphabetical order by
    first names. Adam and Emily are first."

While Adam and Emily went to the cage,
   Mr. Rose continued. "The baby gerbils
   are not the only new addition
   to our class today," he said.
"Are we getting a new kid?" Justin asked.
"No, not a new student," said Mr. Rose.
   "But something new to study."
"Is it animal or vegetable or mineral?"
   asked Kelly.
"It must be *animal*," said Jennifer, "because
   this is Pet Day."
"Right!" said Mr. Rose. "We not only have
   four new gerbils today. We also have
   six other pets."
   Mr. Rose reached into several different boxes.
   First he held up a brown animal with a long tail.
   "This is a kangaroo rat."
   From another box Mr. Rose pulled something
   called a chuckwalla.
He said, "If it's too hard to say chuckwalla,
   you can just say lizard. When he's scared,
   he gets fat with air."

Then Mr. Rose showed everybody two
    strange-looking creatures.
Desert iguanas.
He explained that *Dipsosaurus dorsalis* is
the scientific name used by people all over
the world for the desert iguana.
"Dipsosaurus dorsalis," Matt tried saying.
    "Sounds like a dinosaur."
"Looks like one, too," said Kelly.
    "Are they related?"
"You'll have to find out," said Mr. Rose.

Finally, Mr. Rose held up a cute,
little, brown pocket mouse.
It was so soft.
So tiny.
So cuddly.
Mr. Rose's class was lucky.
Very lucky.
Their classroom was alive with animals.

"Can anyone guess what all these animals
    have in common?" asked Mr. Rose.
 No one guessed.
"They all live in the desert," said Mr. Rose.
"What are they doing here then?" Justin asked.
"We're going to build a desert," Mr. Rose said.
    "Then we're going to put the animals
    in their new home."
"Isn't that too hard for us?" asked Richard.
"No," said Mr. Rose. "It's not too hard. I'll
    help you. I bought soil, sand, and plants."
"Is that all we need?"
"That's all," answered Mr. Rose.
"When do we start?"
"Right now!" Mr. Rose said.

# CHAPTER TWO
# THE DESERT

Mr. Rose had made a special box.

It was big and deep.

Three of the sides were made of cardboard.

But the front side was clear plastic.

Plexiglas.

Some kids helped Mr. Rose put the box

on a big table near the window.

Mr. Rose called one group at a time
to help him build the desert.
Jennifer and Kelly were first.
They started with the dirt.
It was clean and dry.
They dumped it into the box—
one pail at a time.
It was hard work.
But fun.
"How much do we need?" Kelly asked.
Mr. Rose answered, "A lot. At least a foot.
Otherwise the kangaroo rat won't burrow."
"Burrow?" asked Jennifer.
"Dummy!" said Kelly. "It means he'll dig
a hole and hide in it."
"Don't act so smart!" answered Jennifer.
"You don't know everything!"

Richard, Matt, and Emily added the sand.
They poured it over the dirt.
Richard yelled, "Add a little more here?"
Matt shouted, "Now put some here!"
"I need some more at this end," Emily said.
Pretty soon, all of them were fighting over
who would pour it where.
Mr. Rose said they had poured enough sand.
"Now start mixing the dirt and sand together,"
    he told them.
Everyone liked the feel of the soil
between their fingers.

"Do we have a foot of soil yet?"
    Richard asked.
"Let's measure," said Matt.
  He got a ruler.
  He measured six inches.
  He made a mark, then measured
  two inches more.
  Not quite a foot, but almost.
  Mr. Rose asked, "How much more soil do you
    have to add?"
  Matt was quick with the answer.
"Four inches!"
"That's a lot," said Emily.
"Not really!" said Richard. "This is fun."

"We're ready for the plants now," said Mr. Rose
    He gave Adam and Jamie work gloves.
"Planting cactus isn't easy—because they're
        prickly. I don't want anyone getting stuck."
"I once got a thorn stuck in me," said Jamie.
    "And it hurt!"
"Just watch me plant this one," said Mr. Rose.
    "Then you can do the rest. Carefully."

Adam and Jamie each planted six cacti.
That made a dozen all together.
Mr. Rose planted one.
That makes a baker's dozen!
Thirteen plants.
All ready to soak up the sun near the window.

Sarah, Sally, and Justin had been waiting
a long time for their turn at the box.
But Sarah said, "I don't mind the wait.
Because we have the best job. We get
to put the animals in the desert."
Before Mr. Rose called Sarah's group,
he showed everyone how to hold an animal.
He approached one slowly from the front,
so the animal could see his hand
and get used to it.
He picked it up and held it against his body.
The animal's feet were resting on his arm
and it felt safe.
Everyone was paying close attention.
Nobody wanted to hold an animal
the wrong way.

"Try not to squeeze too hard," said Mr. Rose.

"Even if it tries to get away."

Squeezing could make an animal afraid.

And then it might bite.

Or run away.

"What if it wriggles a lot?" someone asked.

"Put your hand firmly on its back," answered

Mr. Rose. "Firm touching calms an animal."

When Mr. Rose was sure everyone understood

the difference between touching and squeezing,

he called Sarah, Justin, and Sally to the table.

"I get the chuckwalla," said Sarah, who was

proud of herself for remembering its name.

Sarah took the lizard from its box and put it

on her arm, just like Mr. Rose showed the class.

And do you know what?

The chuckwalla wasn't scared.

It didn't puff itself up with air.

Justin opened the box with the two desert iguanas.
The first one was easy to catch.
"It's skin is scaly and cold," said Justin as he
    put it in the desert.
The second iguana scooted around the box.
Justin couldn't catch it.
"It's a crazy iguana!" Justin said.
    "I'm scared to grab it."
"Do you want help?" Sarah asked.
"Yup," answered Justin.
Justin was disappointed he didn't do it himself.
Next time he hoped to be a better lizard-catcher.

The kangaroo rat was pretty big and
easy to hold.
Sally stroked its back.
Then she put it into the desert.
The kangaroo rat saw the iguana and
chased it around the box.
"I hope they learn to get along," said Sally,
as she headed for the the box with the mouse.

Sally held the pocket mouse in her hand.
His claws felt tickly.
His fur felt silky.
His nose wiggled when he sniffed.
The pocket mouse was so soft, so tiny,
and so cuddly, Sally wished she could
hold him for the rest of the day.

# CHAPTER THREE
# WHERE'S THE MOUSE?

"Why are you putting a light in the desert?"
   Jennifer asked.

Mr. Rose answered, "Because lizards need
   both hot and cool . If there's no
   time  for them to get warm, they won't
   eat. And they'll starve."

"I'm starved!" Justin said. "When's snack time?"

"Let's have it now," answered Mr. Rose.

"Then Jennifer can tell her story."

When everybody had finished eating, Jennifer walked to the front of the room.

She thought she had a good story to tell.

It was about her guinea pig.

Jennifer said:

> I have a guinea pig named Mr. Krinkelbine. He has long, curly hair—brown and white— and he's twice the size of a gerbil.
>
> Mostly, he stays in his cage or on the floor. One day I put him on my bed. That was a big mistake. Krinkie fell off the edge and landed on the floor. He lay on his side for a few seconds, then rolled over. He just sat there staring at me. I took Krinkelbine to my mom. She said he looked okay, but we'd better watch him carefully for the next few days. Well, the next morning, he started to limp.

Jennifer held up her right leg and hopped.

Jennifer finished her story:

We took Krinkelbine to the vet's office.
The vet made a splint for his leg and
told us to bring him back in two weeks.

"What's a splint?" Adam asked.

"It's like a Popsicle stick," said Jennifer.
"Krinkie had a piece of wood taped
to his leg."

"What's a splint for?"

"The vet said it was to keep the leg still—
so it could heal," Jennifer answered.

"Just like the splint the doctor put
on my finger when I hurt it playing ball,"
Emily added.

"How's your guinea pig now?" Sarah asked.

"He walks a little funny, but he's fine,"
answered Jennifer.

It was Matt's turn to report.

He put an empty bowl on the table.

"This is my turtle's bowl," he said sadly.

"And this is my turtle's rock."

"Where's your turtle?" someone asked.

"He died," answered Matt.

Everyone felt sorry for Matt.

"What happened?" asked Sarah.

"I don't really know," Matt said. "I gave
him a bath one morning and put him back
in the bowl. Then he died."

"Maybe the water was too hot."

"Maybe," said Matt.

"Did you bury it?" Justin asked.

"No," Matt answered. "My dad said the best
thing to do was to say goodbye and flush
the turtle down the toilet."

"Did you cry?"

"A little," Matt answered.

Mr. Rose said, "We have to be very careful with our pets. They rely on us. Jennifer learned that she has to keep an eye on her guinea pig when he's out of his cage. And Matt's story shows that we shouldn't wash an animal unless we know exactly how to do it."

He saw Matt frown.

"Don't feel bad, Matt. It could be that the bath had nothing to do with your turtle's death. Small animals live much shorter lives than people. And often we don't know why they die."

"I have a dog who's eight. My grandpa says that an eight-year-old dog is like a forty-year-old person," said Jennifer.

"Do you think one of our class pets will die?" asked Matt.

"I hope not," said Mr. Rose.

"But it could happen."

It was Matt's and Kelly's turn
to watch the animals in the desert.
They had pencils and paper so they
could draw pictures and make notes.
"That iguana looks comfortable," said Kelly.
"He made a home for himself between
the rock and the heat lamp."
"The other dipsosaurus dorsalis looks
comfortable, too," said Matt. "On the
shady side of the rock."
"Forget the big words!" said Kelly. "Just say
iguana, like me."
Kelly started to draw a picture of the
iguana warming himself near the lamp.

When the kangaroo rat came around,
the iguana jumped at him.
Shoo!
Get away!
The rat was in the iguana's territory.
Matt, who was small, was happy to see
the little iguana chasing the bigger rat.
"That rat will just have to find himself
    another place," Matt said.
Then Matt thought he would like to hold
the pocket mouse.
He looked for the mouse, but he couldn't
seem to find it.
"Kelly," he asked, "have you seen
    the little mouse?"
"Nope," she answered. "But I haven't been
    looking. I'm drawing."

Matt looked all over the desert.

Behind the rocks.

Under the cactus plants.

In the corners.

When there was no place else to look,
he yelled, "The mouse is missing!"

Yes, the pocket mouse was missing.

And Mr. Rose's class would have to find it.

# CHAPTER FOUR
# LOST AND FOUND

"What do you mean, missing?"
   shouted Jennifer. "It can't be missing!"
"But it is!" Matt insisted.
"You must not be looking in the right place,"
   said Jennifer.
"So come here and look for yourself,"
   suggested Kelly.

Jennifer searched.

So did Emily.

Pretty soon there was a crowd at the box.

"What's going on?" asked Mr. Rose,
who had been busy with another group.

"Matt lost the pocket mouse," said Kelly.

"I did not!"

"Okay, okay, calm down, Matt," said Mr. Rose.
"Are you sure he isn't in his burrow?"

"I didn't think of that," said Matt.

He started to stick his finger down the
pocket mouse's hole.

"Wait!" Mr. Rose stopped him.

"The mouse might bite you."

"Then how will I find him?"

"You'll have to think of another way,"
Mr. Rose said.

Kelly had an idea.

"We could stick a piece of string down
his hole and see if he comes up."

"That might work," said Mr. Rose.

Matt and Kelly decided to try it.

They found a long piece of string
and carefully put it down the hole.

"This is like going fishing," said Kelly.

"I've never fished for a mouse before,"
said Matt.

The string went down.

But the pocket mouse did not come up.

"Maybe the mouse escaped and is hiding
under one of the tables," Adam suggested.
"Or, maybe under a bookcase," said Jamie
as she bent over to check.
"I hope it doesn't go outside," said Richard.
"It might freeze to death."
"I'm sure it hasn't gone that far," Mr. Rose
said. "Let's keep looking."
Everyone in the class searched the room.
Everyone but Sally.
She stood in the corner with her pocketbook
and just watched.

Suddenly a fight broke out by the window.

Justin was pushing Matt.

"You took him!" Justin yelled.

"I did not!"

"The mouse was there when it was our turn
to watch the animals," Justin shouted.

Mr. Rose said, "That's enough, Justin.

I'm sure no one took the mouse.

Everyone knows the pets are for sharing."

Sally felt bad .
She didn't want Matt to get in trouble.
She raised her hand and asked Mr. Rose
to come talk to her in the corner.
"What is it, Sally?" Mr. Rose asked.
"I know where the mouse is," Sally said.
 Her face was red.
"Where?"
"Right here."
 Sally had the mouse all along—
 in her pocketbook!

"Why did you take him, Sally?"
    Mr. Rose asked.
"I wanted it. I've never had a pet.
    I never have any pet stories to tell."
    Sally started to cry.
    Mr. Rose said, "You know what you did
        was wrong, don't you? I'm glad you
        gave the mouse back. Now we can
        all enjoy him."

Sally nodded as she wiped her eyes.

"Maybe, if your parents say yes, you could
take one of the gerbil babies home
when they're older," Mr. Rose said.

Sally smiled. "I'd like that."

She gave Mr. Rose the pocket mouse.

"Now remember, Sally," he told her.
"This is a pocket mouse, not a
*pocketbook* mouse."

Sally giggled.

Mr. Rose always knew how to make
people feel better.

"We found the pocket mouse," Mr. Rose said
    to the class. "Everybody back to your seats."
  Mr. Rose put the mouse back in the box.
  Everyone was glad the mouse was safe again.
"Well, this has been quite a Pet Day," said
    Mr. Rose. "What have we learned about
    animals today?"
"Mammals give birth to live young,"
    said Jamie.
"Be careful with pets," said Justin.
    "Especially babies."
"Small animals don't live as long as people,"
    said Matt.
"Good," Mr. Rose said. "Anybody else?"
"Pets are fun to share," said Sally.
"Right!"

"Well, what should we do tomorrow?"
Mr. Rose asked.

"Don't *you* know?" someone yelled.

"Maybe I do, and maybe I don't,"
Mr. Rose teased. "You'll just have
to wait and see. Class dismissed.
See you Tuesday.

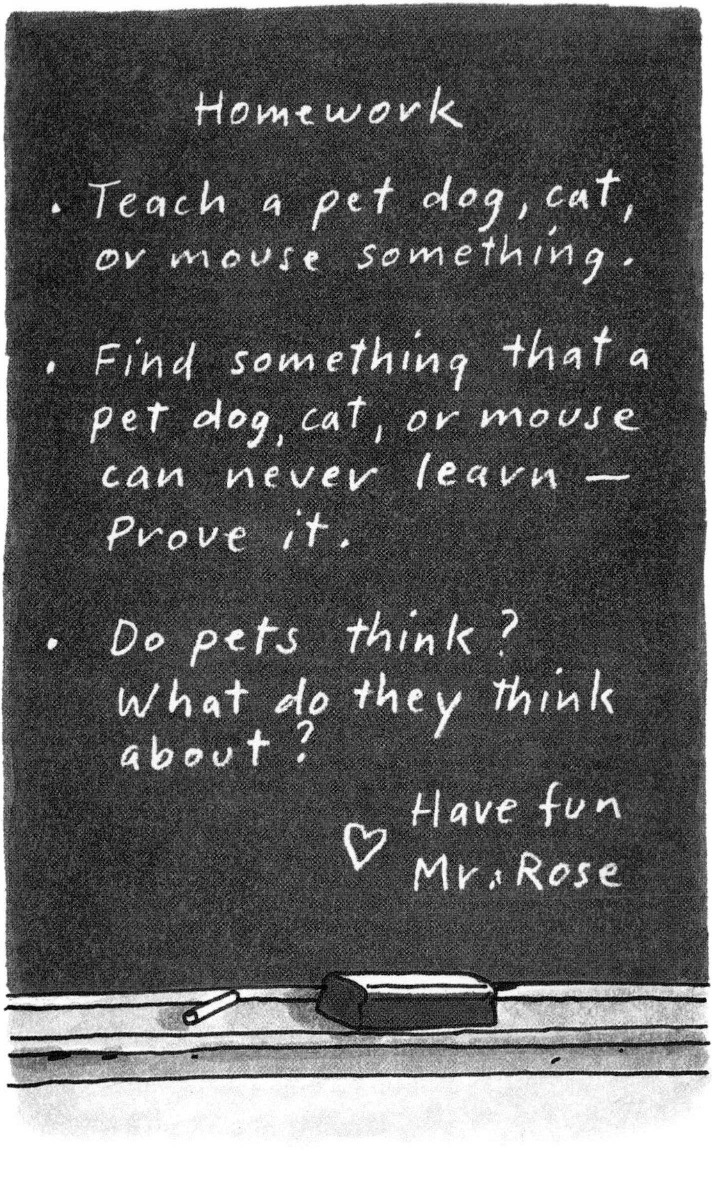
Homework
• Teach a pet dog, cat, or mouse something.
• Find something that a pet dog, cat, or mouse can never learn — Prove it.
• Do pets think? What do they think about?
Have fun
Mr. Rose